This Little Tiger book belongs to:

_____

_____

_____

For Noel, Kayleigh, Gem and Holly
and my very special Dad. Thank you.
~ A M

For Paul with thanks!
~ S M

LITTLE TIGER PRESS
1 The Coda Centre, 189 Munster Road, London SW6 6AW
www.littletiger.co.uk

First published in Great Britain 2005
This edition published 2016

Text copyright © Ann Meek 2005
Illustrations copyright © Sarah Massini 2005
Ann Meek and Sarah Massini have asserted their rights to
be identified as the author and illustrator of this work under
the Copyright, Designs and Patents Act, 1988

A CIP catalogue record for this book is available from the British Library

Printed in China • LTP/1800/1763/1216
All rights reserved • ISBN 978-1-84869-668-6

10 9 8 7 6 5 4 3 2 1

Ann Meek   Sarah Massini

I'm Special,
I'm Me!

LITTLE TIGER PRESS
London

Milo looked in the mirror and sighed
a big sigh.
"Come on, Milo, we're going to be late!"
called Mum up the stairs.
Milo pressed his nose right up
against the cool glass.
"What am I going to be today?"
he whispered to himself.

At school Milo and his friends were playing a jungle game.
"Please can I be the lion?" asked Milo.
"No," said Clare. "You're not strong enough to be king of the jungle."
So Milo was a rather sad monkey.

When he got home Milo peered into
the mirror.
"Who can you see?" asked Mum.
"A monkey," replied Milo quietly.
"Lucky you," said Mum. "How fantastic
to be able to swing through the trees
with all your monkey friends."
"Oh yeah!" said Milo, grinning and
making monkey faces at his mum.

The next day the children were
playing pirates.
"Please can I be the captain?"
asked Milo.
"No," said Ben. "You're too short.
The captain has to be tall."
So Milo had to be a deck hand.

"What's wrong?" asked Mum that evening.
"I wish I was tall, like a pirate captain,"
said Milo.
"I think you are just perfect," said Mum.
"Just right for climbing to the top of the
sails to be the look-out."
"Wow!" said Milo, smiling. "I never
thought of that."

The next day the children were playing
princes and princesses.
"Please can I be a prince?" asked Milo.
"No," said Jason. "The prince is
handsome like me."
So Milo was an unhappy knight.

Later that afternoon Milo gazed into the mirror. "Hello there, Milo," said Mum. "Who can you see looking back at you?"

"I can see a knight," said Milo.

"Terrific!" said Mum. "All that shining armour and you must be brave because only the bravest men are chosen to be knights, you know."

"Really?" said Milo, a little surprised.

"Definitely," said Mum.

"Cool!" said Milo, pretending to fight a dragon.

The next day the children were playing spacemen and aliens.
"I'd like to be an astronaut," said Milo, excited.
"No!" said Eloise. "Astronauts can't wear glasses because their helmets wouldn't fit."
So Milo was a little green alien.

Back home Milo gazed at his reflection in the mirror. "Do I look like an alien?" he asked. "You look just like you," said Mum. "Two eyes, a nose and a mouth, but different from everyone else and that's what makes you special, that's what makes you my Milo."

Mum put her arms around him. "And anyway, aliens are so lucky to be able to bounce around in space speaking a secret alien language."

"That's true," Milo smiled. "*Bling, bling, yook, yook,*" he said, bouncing around his bedroom, trying to catch his mum.

The next day the children
were playing under the sea.
"I'm going to be a shark," said Alex.
"I know what I'm going to be!"
said Milo. "I think I'd be a
good stingray, hiding in the
sand and swimming out
and surprising people and
making them JUMP!"
The children all stared at Milo . . .

"Great idea," said Ben.
"Brilliant!" said Clare.
"Can I be one too?"
asked Alex.
Milo smiled from ear
to ear, and ALL the
children played stingrays
under the sea for the
rest of the day.

"That was a great game, Milo,"
said Ben. "Let's play it again
tomorrow."
Milo smiled the shiniest smile
he had ever smiled.

When he got home that day, Milo
looked carefully into his mirror to
see if he had changed in any way,
but of course he hadn't.
"Mum was right," he said, "I can be
whatever I want to be – I'm ME!"
And in the mirror Milo's reflection
looked back with a huge, shiny smile!

More fabulous books
from Little Tiger Press!

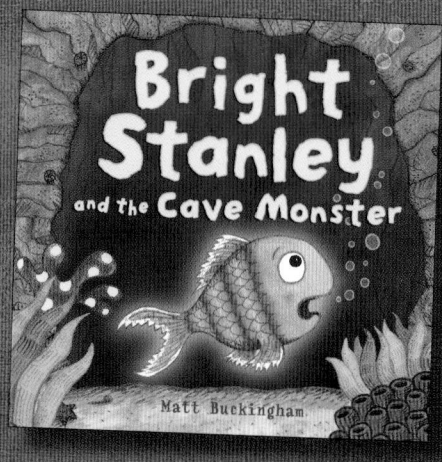

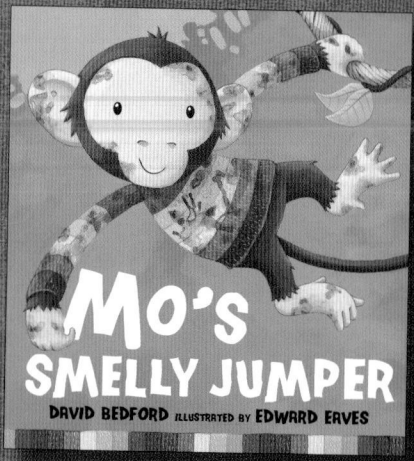

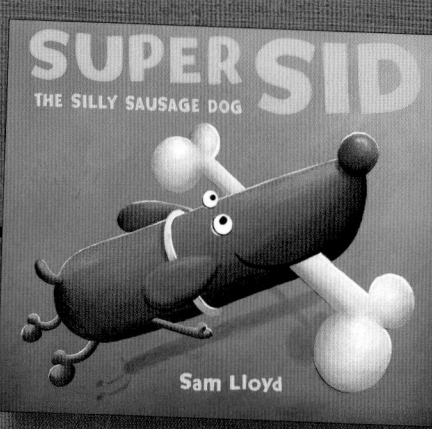

For information regarding any of the above titles
or for our catalogue, please contact us:
Little Tiger Press, 1 The Coda Centre,
189 Munster Road, London SW6 6AW
Tel: 020 7385 6333
E-mail: contact@littletiger.co.uk
www.littletiger.co.uk